When Broccoli Invaded Candy Land

By

Jasmine Malaya Ray

AuthorHouse™
1663 Liberty Drive
Bloomington, IN 47403
www.authorhouse.com
Phone: 833-262-8899

Because of the dynamic nature of the Internet, any web addresses or links contained in this book may have changed
since publication and may no longer be valid. The views expressed in this work are solely those of the author and do
not necessarily reflect the views of the publisher, and the publisher hereby disclaims any responsibility for them.

Any people depicted in stock imagery provided by Getty Images are models,
and such images are being used for illustrative purposes only.
Certain stock imagery © Getty Images.

This book is printed on acid-free paper.

ISBN: 978-1-6655-5341-4 (sc)
ISBN: 978-1-6655-5340-7 (e)

Library of Congress Control Number: 2022903804

Print information available on the last page.

Published by AuthorHouse 02/26/2022

authorHOUSE

Have you ever seen broccoli talk?... Because in this story you will!! I want to talk to you about a place that I miss a lot, it is called Candy Land, but this story does involve broccoli... Wait! Please don't close this book... or I will come to your house and eat all your cookies!...

Long ago, there was a beautiful princess named Stephanie. Princess Stephanie had a wonderful life, but one day something terrible happened. Thankfully, she saw it coming. It was broccoli, and the broccoli was coming straight for her and all of Candy Land.

Princess Stephanie knew exactly what to do. So jumping right into action, she shouted throughout Candy Land; "Every candy, listen up! There is an army of broccoli coming our way, so make it hard for them to get in and remember to stay calm."

Every candy got to work right away and built a candy wall. They worked so hard that they began to produce a very powerful sugary candy scent, so that army of broccoli knew they were a force to be reckoned with.

The strong candy scent was a dead giveaway. However, it was a sweet trick to lure the army of broccoli closer to the candy. All the candies built traps all around their village just beyond the candy wall. This was done in order to capture the army of broccoli. (Oh, I almost forgot. If you want to know what an army of broccoli looks like, picture a big blob of green mush. No offense broccoli.)

Once the army of broccoli broke through the candy wall and entered Candy Land, every candy hid. Well, almost every candy. Princess Stephanie's favorite candy, a large tub of strawberry taffy, was in the middle of the floor.

Princess Stephanie grabbed the taffy and rushed down FIVE FLOORS of her candy castle IN UNDER ONE MINUTE! She ran down those isomalt stairs faster than a chocolate cheetah could sprint! Her heart was pounding faster than licorice lightning. Boom-Boom! Boom-Boom! She slammed the cinnamon graham cracker doors behind her as she reached the bottom floor of her candy castle. The entire community of Candy Land met her there. Good thing that every candy had already set out traps for that fast approaching army of big green mushy broccoli. (Again, no offense broccoli.)

The first trap behind the candy wall was quick sugar, so that the broccoli wouldn't be able to move. The second trap, was a thick pink fog of bubble gum so that the army of broccoli would get all sticky and not be able to see ahead of them. The final trap was a large patch of yellow cotton candy. It was spread out over a huge deep pit filled with rock candy gravel. This would be the perfect trick for when the army of broccoli approached, they would fall straight in.

Princess Stephanie grabbed her favorite candy, a large tub of strawberry taffy, just in time. They were getting close. She could now smell the sweet air of Candy Land being overcome by the smell of mushy broccoli. (Just so we are clear, no offense broccoli, really.)

She knew the army of broccoli was upon her. She ran to a secret area on the bottom floor of the candy castle into a secure room made of assorted treats.

"Why were you outside of the candy cubbard and sitting in the middle of the floor, my sweet large bucket of strawberry taffy? You are my favorite candy and you are in big trouble missy!" Princess Stephanie said in breathless distress.

Princess Stephanie's favorite candy, replied, "Taffy is not meant to be contained, I felt crowded in that cubbard, I wanted to stretch out."

Meanwhile, as the army of broccoli approached closer into Candy Land, they all became very puzzled about what they were seeing as they entered. The army of broccoli's leader was the bossy one of the group. His name was Commander Bossy Broccoli, no surprise there...

Commander Bossy Broccoli began to scream "Why aren't you broccoli moving forward to invade Candy Land? It's not a big deal, come on, let's push past this candy wall and charge!" Then, the army of broccoli marched themselves right past the wall and into the first trap that the candies set out for them.

Almost the entire army of broccoli didn't realize they were caught in the trap until they were up to their florets in quick sugar.

The rest of the broccoli who managed to get past the quick sugar were caught in the fog of pink bubble gum. Only one broccoli managed to get out and it was the bossy one. Commander Bossy Broccoli carefully crept forward after escaping the second trap, looking out for more candy traps ahead and leaving the rest of the broccoli behind mischievously shouting; "I'll come back for you, once I'm king of Candy Land, Hahaha!"

Commander Bossy Broccoli kept marching. However, his march was cut short when he got stuck in the final trap, yellow cotton candy over a deep pit filled with rock candy gravel. Commander Bossy Broccoli fell straight through the yellow cotton candy surface and down into the deep pit of rock candy.

While Commander Bossy Broccoli was stuck in the cotton candy trap filled with rock candy, all of the candies in Candy Land had an emergency meeting.

"Okay we have to be very quiet because we don't know where the army of broccoli is and judging by the strong smell, they are close and could be listening to our every word."

Princess Stephanie whispered. "When do you all think we will be safe to make our way back into our beloved Candy Land to see if our traps worked?"

A coconut macaron leaned forward and replied "Honestly, I really don't know, but we can't expect anyone to do it for us, we will have to take a risk and make our own way back in... Get it, make-our-own? Mac-ar-on? Ha!"

"Coconut Macaron, no time for jokes, what do you mean that you don't know? Our beautiful Candy Land is on the line." Princess Stephanie said.

"Yeah, we should be out there fighting, not hiding and being sitting ducks!" a purple marshmallow peep candy chick chirped angrily.

The crowd of candy that was gathered at Princess Stephanie's candy castle bottom floor, started to chatter anxiously. "Calm down every candy.", said Princess Stephanie "I'm sure that every sweet little thing will be just fine."

"Be fine? We are stuck in a room with broccoli on the loose. What kind of princess are you?"; a sour jelly bean snarled.

Then a chocolate brownie replied gently to the sour jelly bean. "Relax, you know that being loud and negative is not going to help anyone, don't you sour jelly bean? Now, where is Princess Stephanie? Princess Stephanie... Princess Stephanie?"

Princess Stephanie was outside on the lower balcony of her candy castle looking out into Candy Land. She said to herself; "They are right. I'm not fit to be just a princess. I am fit to be brave, positive, kind, and most of all, loving. So I am going to be all of those things and be the best person I can be."

Every candy was very surprised when Princess Stephanie stood up for herself and realized they were being rude and mean. They all apologized.

Afterwards, Princess Stephanie decided to face the army of broccoli. She grabbed her favorite candy, a large tub of strawberry taffy, and went back up the five floors of isomalt stairs in her candy castle to search for the green mushy mob. All of the rest of the candies followed.

Princess Stephanie found all the broccoli stuck in each of the traps that the candies set out for them. She promised to set them free on one condition. They would have to conform to the rules of Candy Land.

1. Bring joy to others
2. Smell sweet
3. Taste delicious

All of the broccoli agreed except, you know who, Commander Bossy Broccoli. "We want to stay here and be ourselves, disgusting and smelly. (As mentioned earlier, no offense broccoli.)

We don't bring others joy either!"; shouted Commander Bossy Broccoli, still stuck at the bottom of the rock candy pit.

Princess Stephanie told Commander Bossy Broccoli that if he and the army of broccoli did not comply, they would be taken into candy custody.

"No, I refuse." said Commander Bossy Broccoli. All the other broccoli caught in the candy traps began to complain in disapproval of Commander Bossy Broccoli's decision.

"I'm sorry but you are all under arrest and will stay in your candy traps until you agree to the rules of Candy Land." Princess Stephanie said.

"WHAT?! WE DON'T WANT TO GO TO JAIL! WE DON'T WANT TO STAY IN THIS TRAP!"; all the other broccoli cried. Princess Stephanie agreed to allow all the broccoli to go free except Commander Bossy Broccoli, who was causing all the trouble.

Princess Stephanie left Commander Bossy Broccoli in the rock candy pit candy trap, but all the rest of the broccoli were free since they agreed to follow the rules.

The broccoli even taught the candy that broccoli actually doesn't smell as terrible as the candies were making it out to be, broccoli makes people happy because it's nutritious, and even though it doesn't taste like candy, it's not bad with a little seasoning.

The candy realized that the broccoli was just fine the way that they were and could stay in Candy Land as long as they were kind and loving.

The candies and the broccoli were looking forward to living together in harmony, especially with Commander Bossy Broccoli under control. So they threw a party together.

But wait, while the candy and the broccoli were dancing together at the party, a candy accidentally knocked over the large bucket of strawberry taffy, Princess Stephanie's favorite candy.

The taffy spilled into the rock candy pit that Commander Bossy Broccoli was in. The trap got so filled up with taffy that Commander Bossy Broccoli was able to climb on top of it and escape.

Oh NO! Commander Bossy Broccoli is now a fugitive on the loose in Candy Land, and Princess Stephanie's favorite candy has spilled!

To be continued...

Lightning Source UK Ltd.
Milton Keynes UK
UKHW051907151022
410462UK00008B/62